DISCARD

Insect Zoo

by SUSAN MEYERS
photographs by RICHARD HEWETT

LODESTAR BOOKS
DUTTON   NEW YORK

A NOTE ON INSECT NAMES

Insects and other animals have two kinds of names, common and scientific. An example of a common name for an insect species is honeybee; the scientific name is *Apis mellifera*. The scientific name is composed of two words. The first is the genus name; the second is the specific name. This system of naming, known as binomial nomenclature, gives a reasonably precise indication of where the animal fits in relation to others of its kind.

For various reasons, a number of species at the Insect Zoo have not been identified beyond their genus name. In these cases, the abbreviation "sp." for species is used. For example, darkling beetles (of which there are a great many, nearly identical, species) all belong to the genus *Eleodes*. The identification *Eleodes sp.* indicates that the beetle in question is a species of *Eleodes*, though exactly which is not known.

TITLE PAGE: **Mexican red-legged tarantula** (Brachypelma smithi)
FRONT COVER: **Leaf-footed bug** (Acanthocephala sp.)
BACK COVER: **Children** (Homo sapiens) **playing on Insect Zoo spider web**
PHOTO CREDIT: page 33, bottom: Leslie Saul

Text copyright © 1991 by Susan Meyers

Illustrations copyright © 1991 by Richard Hewett

Library of Congress Cataloging-in-Publication Data

Meyers, Susan.
Insect zoo / by Susan Meyers; photographs by Richard Hewett.

p. cm.

Summary: Describes, in text and photographs, the San Francisco
Insect Zoo and the many insects that are kept there.
ISBN 0-525-67325-3
1. Insects—Juvenile literature. 2. San Francisco Insect Zoo—
Juvenile literature. 3. Arthropoda—Juvenile literature.
(1. Insects. 2. San Francisco Insect Zoo. 3. Arthropods.)
I. Hewett, Richard, ill. II. Title.
QL467.2.M49 1991
595.7'0074'79461—dc20
90-35177 CIP AC

Published in the United States by Lodestar Books,
an affiliate of Dutton Children's Books,
a division of Penguin Books USA Inc.

Published simultaneously in Canada
by McClelland & Stewart, Toronto

Editor: Rosemary Brosnan Designer: Richard Granald, LMD

Printed in Hong Kong First Edition 10 9 8 7 6 5 4 3 2 1

ACKNOWLEDGMENTS

We are extremely grateful to the staff of the San Francisco Insect Zoo for their help and cooperation with this project. All were generous with their time as well as with their knowledge of the fascinating and highly complex world of insects.

We especially want to thank Leslie Saul, Curator of the Insect Zoo (shown above with a Polyphemus moth); David Herlocker, Insect Zoo Technician; Nicolas Solberg, Insect Zoo Intern; and Tom Turowski, Insect Zoo Technical Assistant.

We also want to thank our editor, Rosemary Brosnan, without whose initiative and enthusiasm this book would not have been possible.

Sri Lankan mantid (*Hierodula membranacea*)

What do you see when you go to a zoo? Some people see lions, tigers, elephants, and giraffes. But visitors to the San Francisco Insect Zoo, in San Francisco, California, see a very different kind of animal life. They get a close-up view of the amazing, sometimes mysterious, and often hidden world of insects.

The San Francisco Insect Zoo was founded in 1979. It was intended as a temporary exhibit within the larger San Francisco Zoo, but it became so popular that the following year it was made a permanent part of the zoo. Now, hundreds of thousands of children and adults visit the Insect Zoo each year to see and learn more about one of the smallest, yet most important, forms of life on earth.

Insects have existed for more than 390 million years. That's about 150 million years before the first dinosaurs and 389 million years before the first humans. There are more than a million known species of insects, hundreds of thousands—perhaps millions—as yet undiscovered species, and billions upon billions upon billions of individuals. More than 80 percent of all the animals on earth are insects. Yet, until recently, no one thought of collecting and exhibiting them in zoos.

The first insect zoo in the United States was opened in 1976 at the Smithsonian Institution's Natural History Museum in Washington, D.C. Other insect zoos are located within the Cincinnati Zoo in Cincinnati, Ohio, and at the Arizona-Sonora Desert Museum in Tucson, Arizona. Insect zoos can also be found in England, Germany, Japan, and many other countries. These zoos provide a unique opportunity for close encounters with the insect world.

One of the most exciting things about an insect zoo is that visitors can see insect life in all stages. They can observe insects mating, laying eggs, emerging from eggs, and molting. Insects, unlike other zoo animals, seem unaware of their human audience. They go about their business much as they would in the wild.

Mexican red-legged tarantula *(Brachypelma smithi)*

At the San Francisco Insect Zoo, visitors can peer into a glass-walled termite nest to glimpse a world they would otherwise never see. They can listen to bees hum in a hive, smell the pungent aroma of stinkbugs, and watch the hunting techniques of predators such as mantids and assassin bugs.

Each afternoon, Petunia, a twenty-three-year-old Mexican red-legged tarantula who is the star of the Insect Zoo's daily Tarantula Talk, provides visitors with a hands-on experience as she patiently allows them to stroke her furry abdomen.

Not all of the inhabitants of the Insect Zoo are insects. Some, like Petunia, are relatives of insects, fellow members of the phylum Arthropoda. A phylum is a large group of animals with sim-

Dampwood termites *(Zootermopsis angusticollis)*

ilar characteristics. The major characteristics of arthropods are a hard outer skeleton, jointed legs, and a body divided into several distinct parts. There are five main living classes of arthropods: crustaceans, arachnids, millipedes, centipedes, and insects. Each is represented at the Insect Zoo.

Crustaceans, like the freshwater crayfish on exhibit at the zoo, are almost all water-dwelling, or aquatic. The majority live in the sea. There are more than thirty-five thousand species of crustaceans, including shrimp, crab, lobsters, and krill, a major source of food for whales and other sea animals. Crustaceans have ten or more legs, two pairs of antennae, and two body parts. Sow bugs and pill bugs, which can be found in damp earth under rocks and logs, are familiar land-living crustaceans.

Arachnids include spiders, scorpions, mites, and ticks. Spiders are among the most popular creatures at the Insect Zoo. In addition to tarantulas like Petunia, the collection includes an ex-

Freshwater crayfish

Black widow spider (*Latrodectus hesperus*)

hibit of black widows. Females of this spider species, found in many parts of the United States, can deliver a deadly bite. The species gets its name from the female's habit of sometimes killing and eating the male after mating.

There are more than thirty-five thousand species of spiders and other arachnids. They have eight legs, one or two body parts, and no antennae. Instead of jaws for chewing food, arach-

Giant African millipede (Archispirostreptus gigas)

nids have mouth parts like soda straws that they use to suck body fluids from their prey. Tarantulas, such as those at the zoo, generally eat insects and other arthropods. But they occasionally devour a small mouse or bird by first injecting the animal with digestive juices to break down its body tissues and then sucking on it until only a small mass of bones, fur, or feathers is left.

Millipedes, which make up the class Diplopoda, are among the most ancient land-living arthropods. Millipede fossils have been found in Paleozoic rocks more than 400 million years old. At present, there are some eight thousand known species of millipedes living throughout the world, especially in the tropics. Most eat decaying vegetation and live in dark, damp places.

A millipede's body is divided into many segments, each having two pairs of legs. The name millipede means thousand-footed, but actually, no millipede species has that many feet. Milly, the Insect Zoo's giant African millipede, has 272 legs. Visitors like the tickly feeling of her many tiny feet walking over their hands.

Centipedes—land-living arthropods that make up the class Chilopoda—cannot be handled safely. They have powerful jaws that can deliver a painful bite. There are more than five thou-

Giant centipede *(Scolopendra hero)*

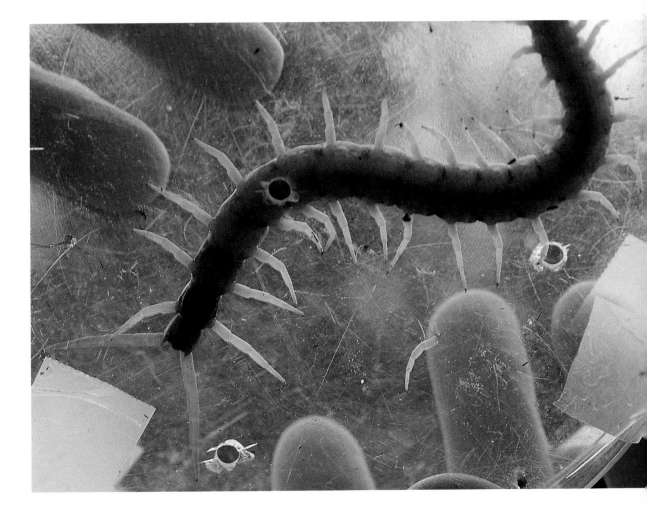

sand known species of centipedes. All are predators, feeding on insects, worms, and other small animals. Most are nocturnal. They rest under rocks or logs during the day and come out at night to hunt their prey.

Centipedes have one pair of legs on each of their many body segments. The name centipede means hundred-footed, but some species have 200 or more feet whereas others have far fewer. If a centipede loses a leg, a new leg will regenerate, or grow to take its place.

By far the most numerous arthropods—and the real stars of the Insect Zoo—are the insects. Hundreds of thousands of species make up the class Insecta, but all can be identified as insects by their six legs, three body parts (head, thorax, and abdomen), single pair of antennae, and in most cases, the presence of wings.

The physical characteristics of insects make them, as a class, the most adaptable and successful animals on earth. They are small in size, so they need little space to live in and little food to eat. Their hard outer skeleton protects them and helps prevent water loss and water absorption. Insect species can live in hot, dry deserts and cold, damp caves. Some live beneath the water in rushing mountain streams or in bubbling hot springs.

Insects' wings help them escape from enemies and travel in search of food and agreeable climates. Insects were the first animals on earth to take to the air. They are the only animals besides birds and bats that can fly.

Some sixty-eight species of insects and other arthropods live at the Insect Zoo. The number of individual animals ranges from six thousand to eight thousand. This is small compared to the total number of insects on earth, but enormous compared to the number of animals living in any ordinary zoo.

Darkling beetles (Eleodes sp.)

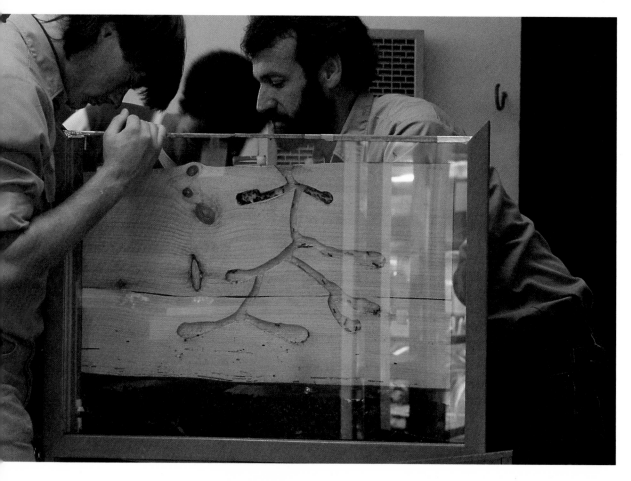

***Repairing an exhibit case housing carpenter ants
(Camponotus sp.)***

Taking care of thousands of living creatures—even such small ones as insects—is hard work. The people who run the Insect Zoo and do this work are trained in entomology, the study of insects.

A curator oversees all aspects of the zoo's operation. Day-to-day tasks are carried out by a team made up of zoo technicians, student interns, and zoo volunteers with a special interest in insects. Together, they perform all the usual zookeeping tasks—cleaning and repairing exhibits, preparing meals, and monitoring the health and well-being of the animals in their care.

The Insect Zoo opens to the public at 11:00 A.M., but long before that the staff is at work. The most important job—one that must be done every day—is feeding.

Preparing meals for dozens of different species of insects and other arthropods is a complicated business. Some need specific types of food that can't be found in the supermarket. Dung beetles, for example, eat the dung, or manure, of large mammals. Every day or so, someone on the staff makes a trip to the water buffalo compound on the larger zoo grounds to collect a fresh supply.

Angular-winged katydid (*Microcentrum rhombifolium*)

Other insects require particular types of plants, which the staff grows in a greenhouse behind the Insect Zoo. Growing food plants, rather than buying them from a nursery, ensures they won't be contaminated with pesticides that could kill the insects.

Some insects eat plants that grow wild on or near the zoo grounds. Katydids thrive on willow leaves. Each morning a staff member hikes to a grove of willows at the edge of the zoo to gather the katydids' breakfast.

Some plant-eating insects can do considerable damage to crops. Yet, many of these insects are themselves food for birds, reptiles, and other insects. Good-tasting insects often protect themselves by blending in with their surroundings. This is called camouflage. A katydid, for example, looks so much like the green leaves on which it feeds that even a very hungry bird may miss seeing it.

Brightly colored insects, on the other hand, often taste bad. Their color acts as a warning sign to predators—who may have tried to eat their kind in the past—to stay away.

Not all insects are so particular about what they eat. Many at the Insect Zoo are general feeders: They eat whatever is available. For these unfussy diners, the staff prepares miniature salads consisting of lettuce, fruit, and monkey chow, a dry protein-rich food that resembles dog biscuits.

People who visit the zoo at mealtime are often surprised to see insects being served much the same kind of attractive, tasty food they might eat themselves.

Darkling beetle *(Eleodes sp.)*

The staff keeps careful written records on all of the animals in its care. Each species has its own feeding and care chart. The person serving the meals marks the charts to show what and when each species has been fed.

In addition to food, insects need water. The general feeders get most of what they need from the fruits and vegetables they eat. Additional water is supplied by misting the exhibit tanks or by adding a dish of water-soaked cotton from which the insects can drink without danger of drowning.

Some insects, once they've finished their regular meal, will settle down to munch on the bodies of fellow insects that have

Domestic cricket (Acheta domestica)

died, usually of old age, in their exhibit tank. Nothing goes to waste in the insect world. In fact, without insects to clean things up—to eat the carcasses of dead animals and decaying plant matter on the forest floor—the world would soon be awash in its own wastes. Then there would be no room for new plants, trees, and animals to grow.

Many of the inhabitants of the Insect Zoo, including all of the spiders, scorpions, and mantids, are predators. Instead of eating plants, they catch and eat other animals for food. Unlike scavenging insects, predators insist on having their dinner live. This means that in addition to caring for large numbers of insects on public exhibit, the staff must raise and maintain hundreds more to be used for food.

The back room of the Insect Zoo is the rearing room. Here, test tubes full of fruit flies, cases of mealworms—the larval form of the mealworm beetle—and tanks of crickets of varying sizes are kept, well fed and cared for, until their time to serve as a predator's meal arrives.

Fruit flies, which are very tiny, are served to young predators. Mealworms are cut up and fed to aquatic insects and crustaceans. Crickets are fed to the spiders, mantids, and other large predators.

Feeding is generally easy. A staff member simply drops a cricket or two into the predator's tank. Sometimes, however, when several predatory insects are sharing a tank, hand-feeding is necessary. Otherwise the smallest ones may not get their share.

Mantids are among the insect world's most successful hunters. They remain absolutely still until their prey comes near and then strike with lightning speed. They are voracious eaters and may feed on one another as well as on other insects. The female often attacks and eats the male during mating.

Juvenile Sri Lankan mantid (Hierodula membranacea)

Predators play an important part in keeping the world's insect population in check. Some farmers and gardeners, recognizing the value of insect predators, use them as a natural form of protection for their crops. They release thousands of ladybird beetles in fields to eat plant-destroying aphids, and encourage other naturally occurring insect predators to live on their farms or in their gardens.

Some insects don't need to be fed by the staff, at least not on a regular basis. The termites, for example, require nothing more than a new plank of wood every few years. The honeybees, one of the most popular exhibits at the Insect Zoo, can leave their Plexiglas hive by way of a plastic tube that extends through the wall of the exhibit room; they fly out of the zoo to find their own dinner.

Honeybee *(Apis mellifera)*

Honeybees are social insects. They live in a colony where different individuals perform different jobs. A honeybee whose job it is to collect food flies from flower to flower, using its long tongue to suck sweet nectar from the blossoms. It stores the nectar in a special part of its stomach. Grains of pollen produced by the flowers stick to its body. The bee brushes the pollen into hairy baskets on its hind legs. When it returns to the hive, it stores the pollen and nectar it has collected in beeswax cells. The pollen will be used to feed the colony's growing bees. The nectar will turn into honey for all the bees in the hive to eat.

Honeybees play a vital role in the fertilization of plants. By carrying grains of pollen from one flower to another, they make it possible for the plants to reproduce. Without bees and other insects to pollinate them, most plants would not exist.

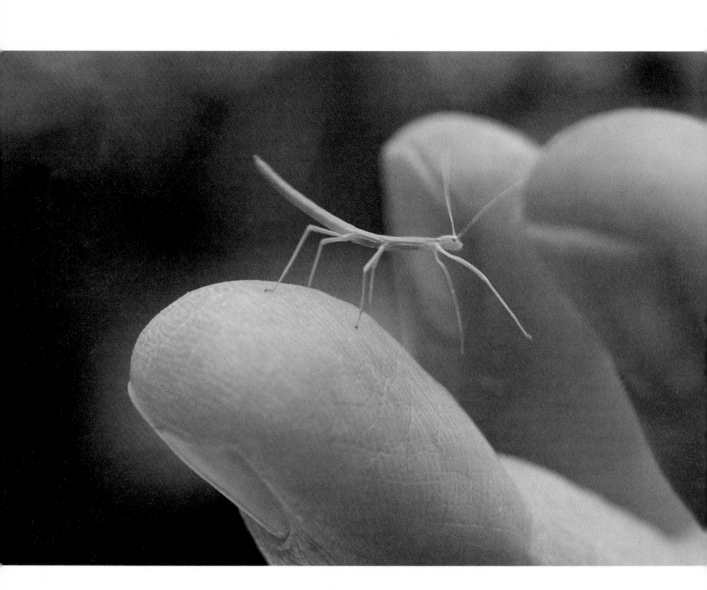

Newly hatched desert walking stick
(*Diapheromera arizonensis*)

One of the things visitors to the Insect Zoo want to know is where the insects and other arthropods on display come from. Many are collected from the wild, in the United States and other countries, by the Insect Zoo staff or by other collectors and entomologists. But in addition, a large number are bred and raised at the zoo. In fact, after feeding, raising young insects is the most time-consuming, complex, and demanding task carried out by the Insect Zoo staff.

The Insect Zoo's back-room nursery holds trays and trays of plastic boxes filled with eggs and newly hatched insects. Tanks of earth contain the larvae of beetles and bugs. Screened cages house mating butterflies and moths. One of the secrets of insects' success is that they are highly prolific. They have many, many offspring. But raising them in captivity can be tricky.

What kinds of conditions does a particular insect need in order to mate? How long do its eggs take to hatch? What food do the young insects eat? These questions are often difficult for the Insect Zoo staff to answer. Many insect species have never been fully studied in the wild, and most have never been bred and reared in captivity. Though staff members read books and consult other entomologists, they often have to experiment to find out what works best.

In the wild, many insect babies, which are tiny and vulnerable, die. At the Insect Zoo, the staff tries to increase survival rates by closely monitoring all of the developments in the nursery. Eggs that have been laid are dated; those that have hatched are counted. Each young insect, no matter how small and insignificant it may seem, is treated as a valued individual.

All insects come from eggs. Usually, the male and female mate so that the female's eggs can be fertilized by the male's sperm. In a few insect species, including aphids and walking sticks, the female can sometimes produce young without a male to fertilize the eggs.

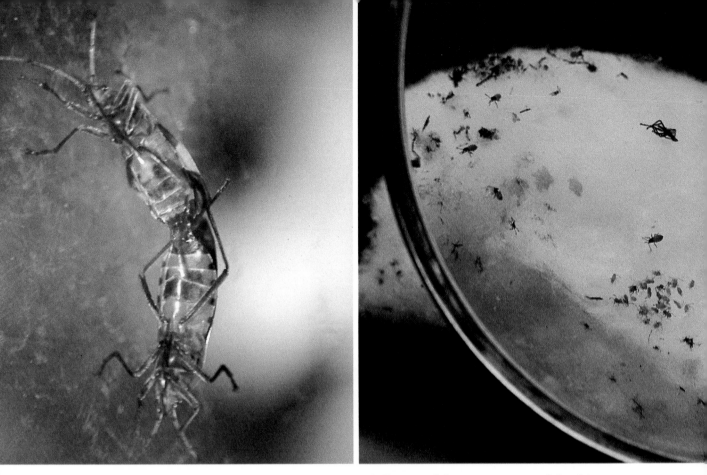

Milkweed bugs mating
(Oncopeltus fasciatus)

Milkweed bug eggs and babies

There are as many kinds of eggs as there are insects. Some are shiny and brightly colored; others are dull and drab. Most people never see insect eggs because they are so small and because the mother insect usually lays them in a hidden place where they will be safe from harm.

In the wild, female milkweed bugs lay their eggs on the soft, white floss inside a milkweed pod. At the Insect Zoo, the staff provides milkweed bugs with cotton, as a substitute for milkweed floss. The bright yellow eggs are laid on the cotton in clusters. In a few days, tiny red milkweed bugs emerge.

Angular-winged katydids lay their eggs in neat rows on the underside of leaves. The eggs are held in place by a sticky substance that hardens as it dries. The Insect Zoo staff gathers the

Angular-winged katydid eggs   **Mantid egg case**

eggs—still attached to the leaves—and stores them in plastic boxes in the nursery. As they hatch, the baby katydids are counted and transferred to other boxes. They live in their nursery boxes, feeding on romaine lettuce leaves, until they're big enough to fend for themselves among the adult katydids.

Female mantids deposit their eggs within a mass of foam that they secrete from their bodies. The foam hardens into a protective case for the hundreds of eggs inside. At the Insect Zoo, mantid egg cases are kept in the nursery in containers labeled by species and date of deposit. After a period of time, usually several months, depending on temperature and other environmental conditions, the eggs hatch and hundreds of baby mantids emerge.

Giant water bug (Abedus sp.)

Perhaps the most unusual egg-laying behavior at the Insect Zoo takes place in the main exhibit room, within the giant water bugs' tank. The female of this predatory aquatic species lays her eggs on the back of the male. The eggs, which are white at first but quickly darken, are attached with a cementlike substance. When all the eggs are laid, the female swims away.

The father water bug carries the eggs on his back for two to three weeks. During this time, he rocks from side to side underwater to keep the eggs washed and aerated. He rests with his back above the surface so the eggs are exposed to fresh air.

When the eggs finally hatch, the father water bug's devotion to his offspring ceases completely. In fact, at this point, he, and

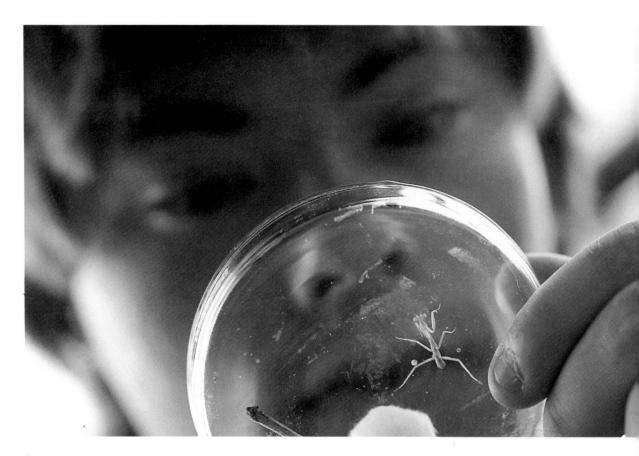

Newly hatched Sri Lankan mantid

the mother water bug as well, are likely to make a meal of any newly hatched babies that don't swim away quickly enough.

Once insects are hatched, they follow either one of two different patterns of growth—incomplete or complete metamorphosis.

Some baby insects look like miniature versions of their parents. As time passes, they grow larger and eventually develop wings, but their basic form does not change. This pattern of development is known as incomplete metamorphosis.

Many of the insects at the Insect Zoo, including the mantids, walking sticks, katydids, and milkweed bugs, go through an incomplete metamorphosis. But the great majority of insects in the world undergo complete metamorphosis. Their form changes completely at different stages of life. With these insects, the baby looks nothing at all like the adult.

At the Insect Zoo, the most dramatic example of complete metamorphosis can be seen in the development of the various kinds of caterpillars that the staff gathers and puts on display each spring. Caterpillars are the baby, or larval, form of butterflies and moths.

Keeping caterpillars supplied with food isn't easy, since they're regular eating machines. But the food they eat is different from the food the adult insect will eat. Each week, pipevine caterpillars consume bushels and bushels of pipevine leaves. Pipevine butterflies drink nectar from flowers. Eating different food at different stages of life is one of the advantages of complete metamorphosis: The insect species can make full use of the food available in a given area.

After a period of time, the caterpillars stop feeding. Each forms a chrysalis, or pupa, inside which amazing changes take place. The caterpillar's whole body is rearranged. When the chrysalis splits, several weeks later, and the fully grown butterfly emerges, the process of metamorphosis is complete.

Changes are always taking place at the Insect Zoo. New insects are collected and put on display. Seasonal exhibits, such as those containing the caterpillars, are dismantled and removed. Each time people come to the zoo, they're likely to see something they've never seen before.

Most visitors are surprised at the sudden appearance of a peculiar ghostlike roach within the tank of Costa Rican wood cockroaches. Where did it come from? Why is it so white? The answer is that the roach is in the process of solving one of the

Pipevine swallowtail (Battus philenor) **caterpillar, chrysalis, and adult**

Costa Rican wood cockroach *(Blaberus sp.)*

major problems of arthropod life—namely, how to grow larger while encased in an armorlike skeleton that remains the same size. The solution is to grow a new, larger skeleton and shed the old one. This is called molting.

When an insect like the wood cockroach molts, its new skeleton—which has grown beneath the old, cast-off skeleton—is soft, pliable, and colorless. The roach pumps the muscles of its abdomen to expand the new skeleton. Chemical changes within the insect's body cause the skeleton to harden and darken. Soon, the newly molted roach resembles its fellow roaches.

34

Molting can be risky for an insect. When it first sheds, it is vulnerable and exposed—a likely meal for a predator. Sometimes, the shedding itself goes wrong, and the insect is crippled or dies. Nonetheless, all insects, whether they go through complete or incomplete metamorphosis, must molt several times before reaching their full adult size and form. Once wing development is complete, insects do not molt again. But many other arthropods continue to grow and molt throughout their entire lives.

Collecting new insects to put on exhibit can take place close to home or far away. Many kinds of aquatic insects are found in a nearby pond. Skimming the water with a net yields an amazing number of species, including whirligigs, water striders, back

swimmers, and scavenger beetles. Traps set at the bottom of the pond or in a stream will catch still more.

Approximately 3 percent of insects spend all or part of their lives underwater, getting the oxygen they need in a variety of ways. Mayfly larvae have developed gills to filter oxygen from the water. Water scorpions extend snorkel-like breathing tubes above the surface. The quick-moving diving beetle carries a handy bubble of air trapped beneath its wings much as a human diver carries a supply of oxygen in an aqualung.

Most aquatic insects live in fresh water. Only a few species live in the sea, which is largely populated by another class of arthropod—the crustaceans.

Each year or two, the curator of the Insect Zoo makes a number of long-distance collecting trips, sometimes traveling with a team of entomologists as far as Southeast Asia or Latin America. Other trips take her to the deserts of the American Southwest.

A desert collecting trip is a major undertaking. Hundreds of containers to hold insects must be packed. The team must also take nets, jars, traps, brushes, forceps, and insulated chests for keeping the insects in good condition on their way back to the zoo. Months before the trip, the staff applies to the United States Department of Agriculture for permits to display the insect species it hopes to collect. The U.S. Department of Agriculture monitors the importation of insects very carefully, since certain insects, brought into a region to which they are not native, could pose a threat to agriculture.

Despite the heat and lack of water, a surprising number of insects and other arthropods live in the desert. They deal with their difficult environment in a variety of ways. Some escape the heat by digging tunnels in the sand. Others have a dense coat of hair to protect them from the sun's rays. Many are nocturnal, or active primarily at night.

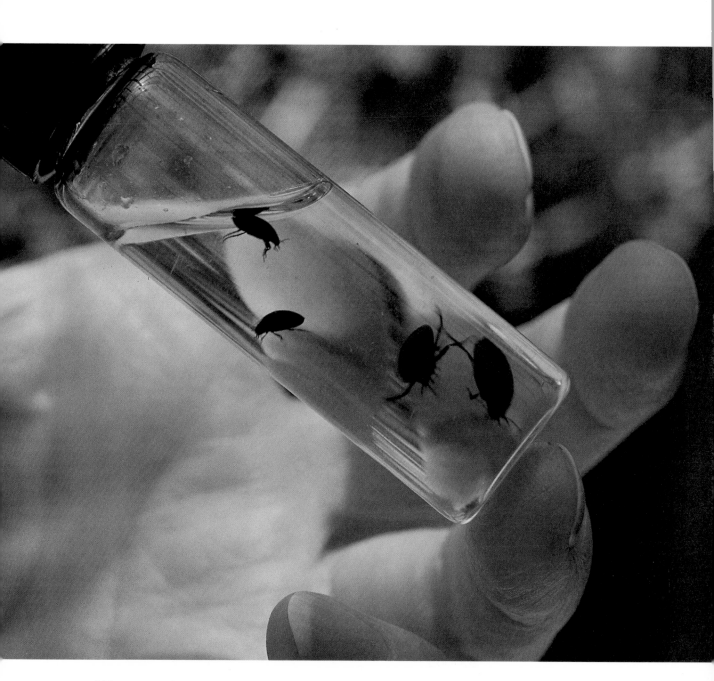

Water scavenger beetles (*Hydrophilus sp.*)

Grey death feigners, a hardy species of beetle found in California's Mojave Desert, are built like armored tanks. Their thick, hardened forewings, which are fused, or joined, so they cannot fly, act as a shield against water loss.

They get their name from their habit of feigning, or playing dead, when startled. In this state, the death feigner shuts off its sensory system and does not respond to any stimuli. This behavior discourages predators looking for a live meal. Other insects, including weevils and dung beetles, use this method of protection, too.

Grey death feigner *(Cryptoglossa verrucosa)*

In addition to collecting insects, the team of collectors gathers bits and pieces of each insect's environment. Interesting-looking rocks, pebbles, plants, and small logs are brought back to be used in the insect's new home.

Soil from where the insect was found is also taken and brought back to the Insect Zoo to be used as a base for the new exhibit. The soil is sterilized by heat to kill any parasites or un-wanted organisms, such as mold, that may be present. Then it is poured into the bottom of a glass-sided exhibit tank. Using the insect's native soil is important, since soil with a salt and mineral content other than what the insect is used to can be harmful. For

American cockroach (Periplaneta americana)

burrowing insects, the soil must also be the right consistency. Then the insect can dig right in and make itself at home.

Lights fixed to the top of the tanks provide the insects inside with warmth. Plants and rocks—or even miniature kitchen cabinets, in the case of the American cockroach exhibit—provide insects with places to hide. Humidity, for species that require it, is supplied by regular misting.

The staff puts a great deal of thought and effort into designing exhibits for the zoo. Each must be as much like the insect's native habitat—where it lives in the wild—as possible. This is partly for the benefit of the insect, which may have very specific habitat needs, and partly for the benefit of visitors to the zoo, who will better understand how an insect lives if they see it in a setting that is like its natural surroundings. The staff hopes that once people realize how closely insects are linked to their environment, they will appreciate the importance of preserving insect habitats in the wild.

Care is also taken to make the exhibit cases escape-proof. Seams are checked for cracks that insects might squeeze through, wire mesh at the top is reinforced, and the tanks are locked with keys available only to the Insect Zoo staff. Such measures are necessary to keep insects, especially those not native to the San Francisco area, from escaping.

Once an exhibit is set up, the staff keeps close watch, monitoring the health and behavior of the new arrivals. Some exhibits are definitely experimental. Can paper wasps be encouraged

Paper wasps (*Mischocyttarus sp.*)

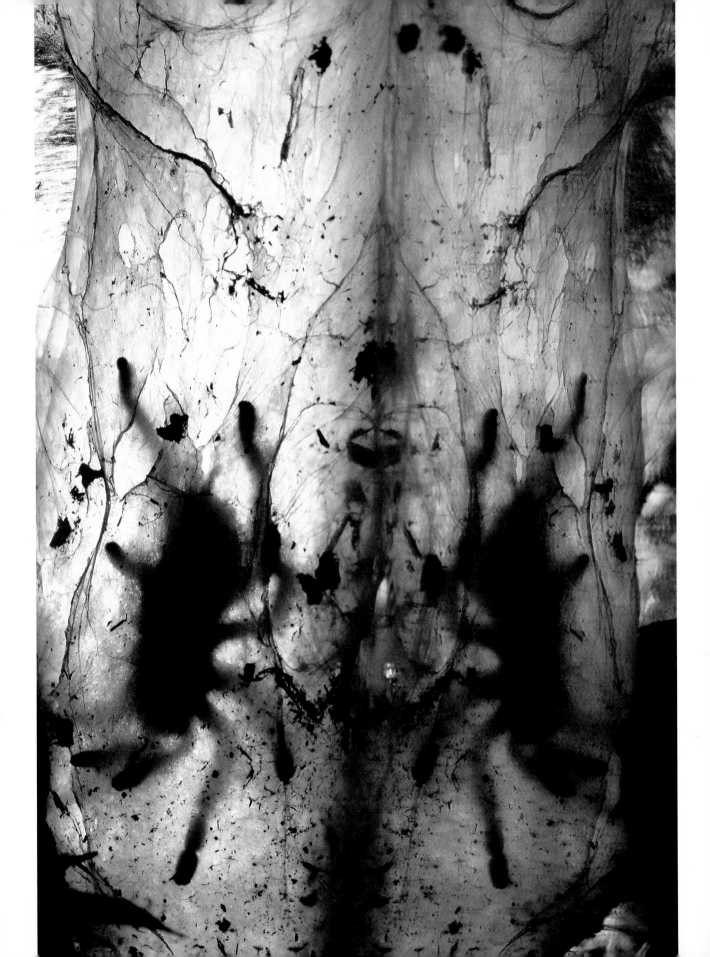

to build a nest and raise young within an exhibit tank? No one knows because no one has tried it before.

Most additions settle in quickly and start going about their normal activities—spinning webs, digging tunnels, building nests. Though insects and other arthropods often carry out highly complex activities, they don't need to think about them, at least not in the way human beings would. Almost everything an insect does is preprogramed, rather than learned. It behaves in a certain way in response to certain stimuli. This kind of automatic behavior is called instinct.

One of the jobs of the Insect Zoo staff is to explain about various aspects of insect life to the people who visit the zoo. Someone is always on hand to answer questions and to take insects out of the exhibit tanks for closer examination. The staff presents slide shows and lectures to interested groups and takes schoolchildren and others on behind-the-scenes tours.

The curator of the Insect Zoo is a frequent guest on radio and television programs. She answers questions and tries to clear up misconceptions and fears about insects and other arthropods. Yes, tarantulas are scary-looking, she says, but they're not dangerous. Their bite is no worse than a bee sting. Don't view insects as pests, she urges, appreciate them as interesting and valuable members of the natural world.

Often people come to the Insect Zoo wanting to know more about insects they have found. The staff helps them identify the insects and lets them use the zoo's reference library to learn more.

Each year, on its anniversary, the Insect Zoo holds an open house called "What's Bugging You? Day." There are games and contests centering around insects, lectures on subjects such as mosquito control and butterfly gardening, and demonstrations by dogs trained as termite inspectors. Before the open house, the staff harvests honey from the Insect Zoo hive so that everyone who attends can have a taste.

Surinam tarantula (Avicularia sp.)

One of the big attractions of "What's Bugging You? Day" is the edible insect buffet. Insects are an excellent and inexpensive source of protein enjoyed by people in many cultures. In Southeast Asia, giant water bugs are deep fried and eaten like potato chips. In parts of Africa, termite larvae make a tasty snack. The Insect Zoo staff serves up chocolate chip cookies studded with dry-roasted mealworms, as well as omelets and dips made with chopped-up crickets. Their aim is to demonstrate that insects could play a vital role in nourishing a world where food is in short supply.

Not everyone is ready to eat insects, but everyone who comes to the open house has a good time. All join in wishing the Insect Zoo a happy birthday and many more years of success.

45

LEARNING ABOUT INSECTS

Would you like to know more about insects? You can learn by reading books and also by keeping your eyes open. Once you start looking, you'll find insects everywhere. Some may live on your family pet, or in your basement, garage, or kitchen. Outdoors you can find insects by turning over a rock, or peeling back the bark on a tree, or looking on leaves, flowers, or blades of grass. To attract insects, you can put out a container of sugar water or smear a ripe banana on a fencepost or log.

The best way to learn about insects is by keeping still and watching them. That's what entomologists do. Use a magnifying glass to get a closer look and jot down your observations in a notebook. So much is unknown about insects, so many aspects of their lives are as yet undiscovered or unexplored, that anything noticed by a careful observer is of value.

The more you watch and think about insects, the more you will be amazed at how successfully they live within their own small worlds. The more you learn, the more you will be impressed by the incredible diversity of life on earth, of which humans, like you, are but one small part.

INDEX

47